The Grinkle Nonk

D E McCluskey

D E McCluskey

The Grinkle Nonk
Copyright © 2022 by D E McCluskey

The moral right of the author has been asserted
All characters and events in this publication,
other than those clearly in the public domain,
are fictitious and any resemblance to real persons,
living or dead, is purely coincidental

All rights are reserved

No part of this publication may be reproduced,
stored in a retrieval system, or transmitted in any form
by any means, without the prior permission, in writing of
the publisher, nor be otherwise circulated in any form of binding or cover other than
that of which it was
published and without a similar condition including this
condition being imposed on the subsequent purchaser.
ISBN 978-1-914381-26-3

Dammaged Production
www.dammaged.com

The Grinkle Nonk

To all the outsiders, and the outcasts everywhere…
Remember, don't try too hard to fit in
It's just not worth it.
Be your own beautiful selves.

D E McCluskey

The Grinkle Nonk

Ha ha ha, hoo hoo hoo,
The Grinkle Nonk is coming for you.
Ha ha ha, hee hee hee,
The Grinkle Nonk'll eat you and me.
He'll grind your bones,
He'll chew your head.
He won't stop biting till you are dead …

Ha ha ha, hee hee hees,
The Grinkle Nonk lives in the trees.
Hee hee hee, har har har,
Tell your mum, you won't go far.
Playing in the forest,
Playing in the stream.
There's no one around to hear you scream…

The Grinkle Nonk
The Grinkle Nonk
The Grinkle Nonk
The Grinkle Nonk

D E McCluskey

1.

IT WAS AN urban myth. A legend passed from generation to generation. Older brothers and sisters would tell the tales in the dead of night, in the silvery light of a full moon, hoping to scare the living daylights out of their siblings. Grandmothers would absently sing the song while changing diapers of their grandchildren, grandfathers would whistle the tune absently as they bounced the same grandchildren on their knees or showing them how to tend to plants in their gardens, or pottering around in their sheds.

It was a silly song, almost nonsensical.

Yet everyone knew it.

No one was sure where it came from, yet everyone had their own versions. Around campfires, in the stark light of torches while wrapped up warm in sleeping bags, during back garden cookouts, where cans of beer were passed around, the tale of the Grinkle Nonk would be relayed.

The Grinkle Nonk

It would be sung without anyone really thinking what the words meant, while concentrating on menial tasks, or if what they were doing scared them. The words had no more meaning than the words of prayers, practiced and muttered for years before bedtime, except for the *deliver us from evil* parts, a lot of scared children *really* meant those bits.

They were just words, spoken or sung with rhythm and rhyme, nothing more. The meaning lost in folklore.

The song told of the Grinkle Nonk. A huge, dangerous, mythical beast with four eyes that lived in the woods and snatched away children while they played by the stream. The consensus was that it was based on tales with at least a modicum of truth. Stories of children missing while on camping trips with their families, snatched during the night, or dawdling behind while hiking, whose bodies were found days, weeks, or maybe even months, later, downstream in various states. As the locals will tell you, anything left in the woods for more than a day was bound to be eaten by something, sooner or later.

The tale of the Grinkle Nonk evolved. It became legend. Some would tell you the name was a mystical Native American word that meant *four-eyed devil in the woods*, others would convince you it was an old Dutch word for the Abominable Snowman, or Sasquatch. But the truth of the matter was, no one knew.

Whatever it was, and wherever it came from, everyone had their own tales to tell. The contents of these tales were diverse. A huge monster or menacing shadow that helped hikers lost in the dense woods find a road that would lead them out of the forest, back to civilisation. Or members of hunting parties going missing, plucked from the group, only to turn up at night as zombies, or ghouls, hungry for souls, or something else just as tasty.

Older boys would make up tales so potential girlfriends would cuddle closer around campfires. Others told it to scare youngsters, setting them up for a big scare that was no doubt coming later, when it was dark, and they were petrified.

No one knew what the Grinkle Nonk was, where it came from, or even if it was real. All they knew was that, because of the silly song, it was coming for them.

2.

THE SUMMER HOLIDAYS in the small town of Noaville, a dwelling on the edge of a great forest, were always warm and dry. The town had been founded, and still thrived to this day, on wood. The main export of the town was lumber. Lumberjacking, carpentry, logging, absolutely anything to do with the trees. The town revered them, respected them, they were the lifeblood of the whole community.

The forest was dense. It was made up of thick conifers, tall proud oaks, aspens, poplars, and many other species of vegetation. Along with the draw of industry to the town, the forest was also an irresistible pull to the children, who over the generations made it their playground. Specifically, the clearing by the stream. If the weather was warm, you would always find children running, playing, picking flowers, swimming, or making dens in the trees and undergrowth. If you weren't playing in the woods during summer, then you might as well not have even existed in the town.

It was where parents came to look for their children when it was time to go home.

Today was no different. The sun was shining, the sky was blue, the scent of phlox mixed with other blossoms blew in the air, making it sweet, and the bee bombs were attracting the attention of hordes of insects, eager to pollinate and spread the species. Children were laughing and screaming as they played the day away, seemingly without a care in the world.

Two girls were twirling a long rope, while a third waited in the wings, ready to jump in and skip the rope in time to the song they were signing. Of course, it was the Grinkle Nonk song. Its gentle rhymes carrying on the air as they laughed and played. They were happy, lost in never ending time, and their fantasies. Nothing else mattered other than having fun, and hopefully not getting your legs tangled in the ropes and falling on your face.

That was when the boys would take notice.

They would stop their games of tag, or football, or war, and would point, laughing at whatever girl was lying in the leaves, spitting them from her mouth. It was the teasing that would drive her to swallow her pride, to get back up, brush herself down, and start again. Maybe with a small, secret smile on her lips, glad at being noticed by the boys.

Everyone was happy, and it was just as it should be, how it had been for generations. However, just lately there had been a strange feeling about the clearing, like they were being watched by someone, or *something*, hiding in the shadows of the trees.

3.

HARPER WAS AN outsider and was slowly coming to terms with this label. She'd known it would be the case, even before her parents decided to pack up from their home in the city, and move … here, to the outskirts of exactly nowhere. In a past life, she had been a popular, sweet natured child, but she knew she was going to have a tough time fitting into her new surroundings, especially in such a rural location.

'Don't be pig-headed, Harper,' her mother scolded. 'Everywhere can accommodate you these days. It's the law.' She'd said this as she unpacked the groceries they'd bought from their trip into their new town. The store they had bought them in hadn't had any accommodation for her. The aisles were far too narrow, the floor was dangerously uneven, and she had taken special notice of the steps leading to the rest rooms. She wasn't being pig-headed; she had become sensitive to these things.

She knew her mother had too.

But it hadn't been her mother who'd received the strange looks in the street, or the sympathetic looks from the older generation. She knew what some of them had been thinking; the likes of her should be kept at home, hidden away from their eyes, not paraded through the streets, brazenly, for all to see. She'd also endured strange and curious attention from babies and toddlers, the ones who'd never seen anyone like her before.

Then, there was the worst indignity. The attention from kids who were the same age as her. She'd felt their eyes crawling all over her, she'd heard the giggling behind hands that covered their faces, and the worst part of all, the whispering.

Back home, in the big city where she had grown up, Harper had been a skateboarder from a very early age. She'd been so much better than the kids her age and had inevitably ended up hanging around with an older crowd. From them, she'd learned tricks and flips and how to navigate the skating parks. She had learned how to survive on the street. She knew its language, its quirks, its limits. She had learned how to be one of the cool kids.

She'd been seen as something of a skateboarding prodigy.

The younger kinds envied her skills, and her social fitting. Even some of the older kids, usually the ones who couldn't quite get their head around the delicate balances, and the nuances of the boards, would ask her advice, and ask her to help them perform the stunts that she took for granted.

The Grinkle Nonk

'I want to be in the Olympics,' she admitted to her parents over dinner. 'Skateboarding is an emerging sport, and I know I'm good enough to compete.'

'Harper,' her dad laughed while ruffling his hand through her hair. She hated that; it made her feel like a child. 'That may be, but they are never going to allow nine-year-olds to compete in the Olympic Games,' he'd say, biting into a triangle of hot buttered toast. 'We'll look into it when you're a little older.'

This had only made her more determined, and she threw herself deeper into her chosen sport. She pushed herself to learn more tricks and more complicated flips. She became reckless, pushing her limits, but all her hard work, and effort, had seemed to be working. She was being noticed for her skills, and her dexterity in the new sport.

But then the inevitable happened.

It was a grey day, and it had been raining the night before. The skate park was awash with puddles, but as it was also unseasonably warm, the surfaces were slick, almost greasy. She was traversing the largest slope in the park, the one that no-one else under the age of twelve would dare attempt. It was the one with the metal banister running along it to grind along, causing cool sparks from the metal of the wheels grinding against the metal of the bar. It was a dangerous stunt, but one she was more than equal to. She had performed this manoeuvrer a million times before and had no reason to think this time would be any different. Her timing was spot on, and her speed had been within normal tolerances on her approach. She was brimming with confidence, aware of the gang of wannabees watching her.

She had been grinning.

What she didn't know was, one of the wheels on her board had worked itself loose. The slick wet of the surface, helped it come away at precisely the wrong time. Just as she was ready to make her jump, and begin the spectacular grind along the metal beam, the wheel buckled, and her trusty board flew away from underneath her.

However, her momentum continued.

It should have been a normal wipe-out, one that happens every single day, hundreds of times, one that she was used to, causing cuts and bruises, and maybe making her limp for a few days, but today was different. Due to the extra slickness of the slope, because of the water, she traversed a little further than normal.

This time she landed on the steps that ran alongside the slope.

She also landed on her neck!

She had lost consciousness, and when she finally woke up, she was in a strange room, lying in a strange bed, surrounded by strange people, using strange words.

She couldn't move her legs. When she looked at them, she saw that they were both in plaster, and elevated up, off the bed, in traction. She had even broken a smile. *Just wait until the other kids get to see this,* she laughed, thinking she would be up, and out of the hospital, within a few weeks, at most. Back in the park, skating harder, and better than ever.

The Grinkle Nonk

That was when the doctors, and her parents began to use strange words. They were words she had never heard before, but had since become unfriendly, and unwanted, constant companions. They were words like *thoracic,* and *lumbar vertebra.* There were even sinister sounding letters and number combos, like *S1 through to S5.* None of them had meant anything to Harper at the time, but now, three years later and living in the armpit of the country, they were her whole life.

She had been confined to a wheelchair ever since.

She had endured extensive surgery, painful physiotherapy, mentally exhausting psychotherapy, but eventually, the doctors, her parents, and even herself, all came to the same, ugly conclusion.

She would never walk again.

To say she had been angry would have been an understatement.

She had been inconsolable, crying herself to sleep for weeks, months, maybe years, but no number of tears, no number of screams of frustration, or exploding anger tantrums were ever going to bring back the use of her legs.

Eventually, she grew to understand, and to even to a degree, accept her fate. All she could do was try her very best to live her life as much as she could.

The surgery, the therapy, and all the psychological analysis had cost her father dearly. That was when she learned another new saying. *Medical Insurance.* This one had become a major part of their lives too, and it was evident that her parents' version of this was woefully inadequate for what had been required to get her better. Her father needed a new job, one with better pay, and a cheaper lifestyle.

That had brought them here.

Wherever *here* was.

'Go and play with the other kids. You know, make some friends. I'm sure there's plenty to do in a town like this,' her mother continued, putting away the last of the groceries.

'There is, if you enjoy the highlife of playing tag, or skipping rope,' she huffed.

'I'm sure the other kids will let you join in. Come on, Harper, you're twelve. I know you've been through more than the average kid your age, but you must want to go outside and play.'

Harper huffed again. She'd tried to make friends, but it was tough, especially in her condition. She hadn't enrolled in school yet, so there had only been limited opportunities to introduce her particular level of cool into a community such as this. So, for now, she was limited to hanging around the woods, on the peripheral of the fun. Watching the kids playing, swimming, running, while she remained alone.

It had been a little over two weeks since they'd moved to Noaville, and she was yet to make even a single acquaintance. She had tried. The other kids had been nice, kind of, but all she could see was the hurdle of her wheelchair putting them off. After all, she couldn't do half the things they took for granted. *I could always make some awesome daisy chains,* she thought, curling her lip.

The Grinkle Nonk

She knew the other kids had noticed her. They'd seen her lurking in the shadows of the trees, watching. She'd been there every day in the hope that one of them might talk to her, offer her their name, invite her into their circle. At this point she would even welcome being invited into the chess, or math clubs, just so she could talk to people her own age. It was infuriating for her, knowing deep down in her heart, *or maybe in my hollow legs,* she thought with a tear welling in her eye, that she was way more interesting, way cooler than all of them put together. None of *them* had ever held aspirations of skateboarding for their country in the Olympics.

She tried not to feel bitter, and not to feel sorry for herself, but it was difficult not to. The transition from cool kid, the one the other kids wanted to hang out with, to outsider, loner, was a difficult one. She wished there was a way she could show them that she was more than just broken legs, metal, and wheels.

She wasn't aware that her wish was about to come true.

~~~

Deep in the woods, deeper than anyone dared to go, four, blood red eyes watched the children play. What they belonged to was real, it was huge, and it was a lot more than just an urban legend.

4.

IT WATCHED AS the children played.

Its multiple eyes were darting in all directions as the children ran, and jumped, and played. It wanted to approach, but knew the songs they sang, the warning their parents gave them. It knew that if it attempted to approach, the screams would begin. Those screams would turn into running, and the stories of the beast in the woods would begin again.

The legend of the Grinkle Nonk would return.

After the tales spread, the men would come. The ones with torches, guns, and angry faces. Shouting men with murder on their minds. There would only be a few at first, but the word would spread, and more would come. They'd continue coming until they found it and hurt it.

It knew all of this because it had happened before, many times. Each time they came, it was with more dangerous, and louder weapons than before.

The Grinkle Nonk

The last time it had barely escaped with its life. It had scurried off into the deep woods, where the men, even with their weapons, refused to follow. There it had stayed, for years. It hid in the trees, scared and alone.

It wasn't stupid. It knew it was the beast in the woods. It wanted to live, deserved to live, just like the humans did. But it knew that if living meant hiding, then it would hide.

So, it hid, and it watched the children play from a safe distance.

What they didn't know, couldn't harm *it*.

5.

'SHE'S THERE AGAIN,' Suzi Benn whispered as she sat on a small blanket set out on the ground. She was opening a large wicker picnic basket her mother had packed for when she took a break from the busy schedule of playing, and *not* looking at boys.

'I know, I saw her earlier,' Prudence Ashe replied, filling three beakers with orange juice from a flask she had removed from her bag. 'She's weird. All she does is sit there, in the trees, all day, watching us.'

'Do you think she might be a child serial killer and is studying us, marking us as her next victims?' Patty Kerr asked, the devilish grin breaking on her face told the other two that she was a strange girl, with a vivid imagination.

'More likely she's after the boys,' Suzi said with an attitude that matched the look in her eyes. She was developing the traits of her sister, Agnes, known through the town as *that little madam,* a title she relished, and one Suzi coveted.

The Grinkle Nonk

'You know, I heard she's in a wheelchair because she was pushed out of a window in the last place she lived,' Prudence said, looking at the other girls, happy with her titbit of information, not even caring that it wasn't true.

'I heard she did it attempting suicide,' Patty added, her eyes wild at the story she had just embellished.

'She was pushed because she had been selling drugs, and it was a turf war,' Prudence continued, glaring at Patty, daring her to make up something better than she had.

'Suicide, because of what she had done in school. Apparently, it was so bad that she just couldn't live with herself anymore,' Patty continued, pulling tongues at Prudence.

Prudence's mouth screwed up into a small white hole, as her eyes flickered while she was obviously trying to think of something else to embellish her fiction.

'Either way,' Suzi added. 'She's obviously a weirdo. All I know is that I won't be talking to her anytime soon, I'll tell you that for free.'

'Me neither,' Prudence offered, trying her best to stay in Suzi's good favours. She had accepted, long ago, that she was destined to be a sidekick, and if this was to be the case, then she was damned sure she was going to be it to the most popular girl in school, or at least her younger sister.

Suzi smiled her best fake smile as she accepted the offered beaker from Prudence.

It was that exact moment that everything changed. The peace, the tranquillity, even the civility of the afternoon was shattered into a million pieces as a terrifying, blood curdling scream ripped through the warm day. It was so loud and so sudden that it caused a flock of birds to take flight from the trees.

Suzi watched them fly off to God only knew where startled birds flew off to, with confused eyes.

At first, she never thought much of it, after all screaming was a regular occurrence in the clearing. However, as she looked towards the football pitch, where the boys congregated, a thought occurred to her. It was terrible thought.

Boys don't scream.

Her breath caught in her stomach as she learned a harsh lesson.

It seemed boys *do* scream.

Her heart began to pound, thudding against her chest as her eyes roamed the clearing, searching for the source of the scream. She needed to see what could have scared the boys so badly, turning them into screeching banshees.

A shadow passed over the clearing. The three girls stopped enjoying their picnic and traced its origin.

Moments later, the boys, all of them, began to sprint past. 'Run!' one of them shouted, looking back at them, panic blazing in his wide eyes.

'The song ...' another screamed in an uncharacteristically high-pitched voice. 'It's true!'

The Grinkle Nonk

'What is?' Suzi asked as he passed at full speed.

'The Grinkle Nonk,' the boy continued, now from a distance. 'It's real.'

'It's here,' another yelled.

Suzi nodded at this information. Even though her throat had turned into sandpaper, and her heart had turned into a heavy metal drummer in her chest, she did her utmost to keep her calm. She wouldn't allow anyone to see her panic. 'I think maybe we should leave too,' she whispered to her ladies-in-waiting.

Her friends were looking to her, as if waiting for instruction. It was obvious they were as scared as she was, but they also didn't want to make a public display of it.

Prudence nodded. Slowly, she put her beaker onto the ground and stood up, brushing the leaves and grass from her dress, as if nothing special was happening. She was almost bundled to the floor by a boy running flat-out, in a mad haste to vacate the area. Even though she was almost spun around in a three-hundred-and-sixty degree turn, she ignored the assault and offered a hand to Suzi to help her up.

Ignoring the offer, Suzi got herself up, closely followed by Patty, who hadn't taken her eyes away from what was causing the ruckus.

'Ladies, we should leave,' Suzi suggested.

Patty and Prudence swapped a look. This was the first time they had agreed on something all day. They both nodded.

Then they ran, all three of them, screaming along with everyone else, all of them heading in the same direction. Not one of them had an idea where they were running to, just as long as it was away from the woods and away from the hideous Grinkle Nonk.

~~~~

Harper was watching everyone run. Why they'd all suddenly started screaming and thundering out of the clearing was lost on her, but she did notice that most of them were looking in her direction as they went.

This did nothing for her self-esteem.

Surely, they've seen a girl in a wheelchair before, she thought. *I know this is a backwater town, but come on, guys, overkill!*

She shook her head as the kids continued to run. Some stopped on the fringes of the forest, just within the treeline, and looked back at her. Even from a distance, she could see their pale faces, their wide eyes.

'It's only me,' she shouted, waving towards them. 'It's just a wheelchair, its nothing to be afraid of.' She banged on the large wheels at the back, just to make her point.

The kids watching her were jumping and shouting, obviously trying to get her attention.

What is the matter with them? They know I can see them.

Then something hit her.

It was a thick, vile stench.

It reminded her of the stink when she used her straighteners for too long and it burnt her hair, but it also had an underlying, lingering nastiness to it, too. It reminded her of sewage.

The Grinkle Nonk

Once, back when they lived in the city, the nearby river had burst its banks after a particularly bad spell of rain, and all the sewers had flooded, turning the streets into a fast-running river. This smelt like that. Grey water they had called it. Even the thought of it made her balk, as she did, she fought hard to stop the inevitable involuntary retches.

That was when she realised there was a shadow behind her. She hadn't noticed that the sun had been blocked out of the sky, mostly because they were in the woods, but also because she had been watching the mass exodus with such rapture. Now that she was alone, she could see how dull the day had gotten. How the birds had all stopped singing in the trees, and there were no rustling sounds beneath her wheels of animals foraging for grubs in the undergrowth. There was only the shadow, the stink, and … now that she thought about it, there was a deep, rhythmic growl too. It sounded like a giant with a bad chest infection, trying its best to breathe.

It was coming from behind her.

Suddenly, despite the warmth of the day, she was cold; so very cold. She could feel it creeping through her bones, up her useless legs, tickling her stomach, and sticking sharp needles into her eyes. The chill had crawled everywhere. She even thought she could feel it in her wheels, even though she knew that didn't make any sense at all.

Her pulse quickened. It thumped in her ears as the rock drummer controlling her heart was now headlining in her brain and was gearing up to play the mother of all drum solos.

The palms of her hands were wet, and as she grasped at the grips on the tyres of her chair, they slipped. She swallowed, it wasn't easy to do as her throat felt as if it had closed over, she shut her eyes tight, and tried to grip her wheels again. Colours blurred and merged behind her eyelids, causing her own personal firework display with every thump of her heart. She opened them again, and instantly regretted it as pain surged through them. Luckily it was only the sting of sweat, dripping from her soaked hairline. Her pulse was in her temples, her ears, her arms. She grasped the wheels again and her hands slipped a second time. She didn't want to turn her head, just in case whatever it was behind her noticed her moving and decided that a young girl, in a wheelchair, might be something new it wanted to eat today. Her eyes flicked towards the ground. One of her wheels had become stuck between two thick roots. On any other day, it would just be a matter of clearing the obstruction away, or bouncing the wheel over it, but today, it was the most impossible deed in the whole entire world. Curing world hunger, or even poverty seemed like a trifle when pitted against getting her wheels out of the tangle and getting away from the stinking, panting *thing* that was blocking out the sun.

She couldn't help turning her head.

Slowly.

Her eyes grew wide, and her blood froze as she struggled to grasp the reality of what exactly it was behind her.

It was difficult to look at. It was just too big, too unreal to fathom. It was impossibly huge, and ugly, not to mention too terrifying for her

The Grinkle Nonk

brain to comprehend. It's four, blood red eyes looked at her. She could see all of them moving, independently of each other.

On top of its head stood two large, dangerous looking antlers. At first, she thought it was covered in twigs and leaves but she soon realised it might have been fur, bristles, or even spines. However, it wasn't what was covering it that was causing her current mental issues. It was its mouth, or more specifically, its teeth. They were like plaque covered tree trunks. They were dirty, sharp, but most of all dangerous. Its small nose was a snout, like the ugliest pig she had ever seen in her life. Its four eyes, each as big as her hand, were droopy and blood red, but they shone with an intelligence she might otherwise have thought impossible. It was standing upright, its powerful legs were covered in the same spines, or fur, as the rest of its body. Its arms were heavily muscled, and its broad shoulders, and terrible hump on its back, heaved with every slow pant of its disgustingly warm breath.

Its hands were defined by its claws, but she could see thumbs, meaning this beast was capable of dextrous tasks, making it even more dangerous than it had first seemed.

Harper felt the need to gulp, but whatever this thing was, it had stolen all the saliva, every little bit of moisture from her body, making her throat too dry and too sore, to function correctly.

Its eyes flicked, regarding her, and she watched, transfixed, as a thick spindle of drool dripped from its mouth.

Another low growl issued from somewhere deep within its bulk.

She wanted to grasp her wheels and spin out of this place, out of its line of vision, out of its reach. If her wheels failed to do what they should, again, then she was ready to fling herself from the chair, and crawl if needs be. She would do anything to get away from this ... *thing*!

She'd heard the other kids talking, and singing, about something called the Grinkle Nonk. A few of the adults had mentioned it too, but she had dismissed the whole thing as a silly story, and the people spreading it, even more silly for giving the legend any credence.

But now, here in the woods, she was suddenly alone with it. The impossible urban myth was standing before her in all its dangerous, hellish glory.

It grunted.

She jumped.

She flapped at the wheels again in the vain hope they might have miraculously untangled themselves.

They hadn't.

It grunted again; this time allowing it to trail off into a low growl that had more bass than disco. She closed her eyes. She tried to remember all the good times she'd had in her short, short life. Suddenly she was back in the park, in her hometown, skateboarding with her friends. She was laughing and joking as the warm air of the afternoon ran its fingers through her hair. She could see the faces of her mother and father, smiling at her. She could even see her cousins, who she'd never really gotten along with. 'I love you all,' she whispered, tearfully accepting her terrible fate.

The Grinkle Nonk

'Hullo!'

'Is that you, St Peter?' she whispered, expecting to see Heaven's Pearly Gates, complete with a long haired, bearded Saint Peter, ushering her inside, when she opened her eyes.

'Erm, no. I... I don't think so,' the gravelly voice replied.

She opened an eye, just the one. She didn't think her brain would be equipped to handle the terror of looking upon the Grinkle Nonk up this close with both eyes. Slowly, the world swam into something resembling focus.

The beast was still there.

She snapped her eye closed again, wincing, waiting for the fatal attack, the one where it opened its huge, ugly mouth and swallowed her up, whole, wheels and all.

But nothing happened.

All there was, was more heavy breathing and a continuation of the foul stench that must have been the thing's breath, although she was getting used to that now, but there was no attack. She opened one eye again, the other one this time, just to see if the previous one had been deceiving her.

It hadn't.

The beast *was* still there. Only this time, it looked a lot less ... beastly.

Its huge, clawed hands were twiddling.

Have I got that right? she thought, taking another look. *Are they twiddling?* She had been right, they were twiddling. Its face no longer looked fierce. It was now, dare she even think it, *sad looking!* This transformation gave her the courage to open both eyes. Working as a team, they confirmed what the single one saw. Yes, it was an enormous beast; yes, it was fierce with dangerous weapons in its mouth and on its hands; yes it had four intelligent, red eyes, and antlers, but it looked sad, longing, and maybe even lonely.

'Why … why haven't you run away, like the others?'

The words were difficult to understand at first, as the voice was mostly a growl and a series of grunts, but somehow, she understood what it was trying to say. She couldn't quite believe this thing was talking to her. 'What?' It was less of a word, more of a gasp, but it was all she could think of saying. In truth, it was probably all she could push out of her mouth, as her fear, coupled by all the adrenalin rushing through her body, had stolen all the breath from her chest.

'Why haven't you run away? Like the others,' it repeated.

Her head throbbed, her stomach bubbled, but she felt like she needed to answer the question. 'I'm… in a wheelchair,' she whispered.

'A wheelchair?' it asked, cocking its enormous head.

She nodded. Her hand went slowly to the large back wheel and tapped it. 'A wheelchair.' All the beast's eyes looked to where she was indicating, her heart slowed to something resembling a normal pace. 'I can't walk, or run, like the others,' she explained.

The monster leaned closer. Its eyes roaming over the chair. She flinched as it reached out a claw and touched the grey wheel. It was so strong, that the chair jerked, violently at its touch.

The Grinkle Nonk

'Why?' it asked.

She couldn't believe she was having this conversation. 'There was an accident,' she answered. Her heart almost melted as the beast's forehead creased.

'An accident?' it grunted.

She nodded. 'Yeah, an accident. So, when the other children run and play, all I can do is sit and watch.'

All the monster's eyes widened, and it stood upright. She looked at it, and only then did she see just how huge it really was. She swallowed; wincing as her dry throat clicked.

'That's what I do too,' it whispered. At least Harper thought it was a whisper, or as close to one that this thing could manage.

It was her turn to be confused. 'What?'

'While the children play,' it grunted. 'I want to play too. But they're scared of me. I'm the beast, they shout as they run.' The Grinkle Nonk bowed its head. 'That's when the men come. Men with fire and sticks that bang. They hurt.'

Harper's eyes were wide, but she was squinting at the same time, a physical impossibility, but that was how it felt to her. 'You ... you don't want to eat us?' she asked, her heart thumping again.

It gave her a look that made her think she was the beast in this situation. 'Eat? You?'

She swallowed again, wishing she hadn't asked the question, but nodded slowly.

'Is that what they think? That I'm going to eat them?'

She was still nodding.

Its eyes widened even more, four pupils growing large enough for her to bathe in. Tears were welling within them. Harper marvelled at the amount of water caught within its eyelids, it looked enough for her to swim in.

'Is that why they run?' The beast sniffed, breathing a shaky breath.

Harper's heart did melt then. She felt it liquidising in her chest. This wasn't a monster. This wasn't a beast. This was a child. A child who just wanted to play. A lonely child who wanted friends to spend time with.

They were the same!

They were both lost souls just searching for a connection. Outsiders. The ones who didn't fit in with the norm. An affinity for this beast was forming within her. It was searching for somewhere to belong, just like she was. 'My name is Harper, Harper Walsh. What's yours?' she asked, holding her hand out to the wretched thing.

As the massive eyes looked at her hand, something changed. It was a special moment, a joining, a team coming together, maybe even a friendship forming.

'I'm the Grinkle Nonk,' it growled, shrugging. It pointed one of its massive fingers at her outstretched hand, she gripped it, and they shook.

~~~

The Grinkle Nonk

Some of the braver children, including Suzi, stopped running when they noticed Harper couldn't get away. They wanted to help her, to get her out of the clearing, to save the poor, stricken girl from the monster, but Suzi stopped them.

'You can't go back there,' she implored. 'You'll be as dead as she'll be within a few minutes.' As she watched the beast advancing on the unsuspecting girl, a small, inquisitive scowl grew on her face. 'What *are* they doing over there?' She asked, more to herself than to the others gathered around her, also watching what was occurring in the clearing. None of them quite believing what they were seeing.

'They're talking,' one of the boys replied.

'Talking?' Suzi hissed. 'That can't be right. She should be being torn apart right about now, limb from limb. The only thing left of her should be that wheelchair.'

'Well, that's not what's happening,' another boy, a tall boy, the one she'd more than a little bit of a crush on just lately, added. 'It looks like she's making friends with the thing.'

Not on my watch, she thought as the Grinkle Nonk lifted the girl, complete with her chair, effortlessly from the trap they were caught in. Then the two of them disappeared into the woods together, holding hands. Suzi turned away from the sickening scene, her mouth pressed into a thin, white, angry line.

6.

THE NEXT MORNING was just as beautiful as the one before. Harper was up and had helped herself to breakfast even before her father had gotten to the table. 'Hey there, beautiful,' he said, scuffing the top of her head. 'What's got you up so early?'

With a small drip of milk dripping from her chin, she looked up from her cereal. She was grinning, almost from ear to ear. 'I'm meeting a friend,' she mumbled through a full mouth, wiping her chin.

Her father's eyes widened. 'A friend, eh? Well, that didn't take long.' He smiled as he sat next to her, pouring himself a bowl of cereal. 'So, who's the lucky person?' His eyes narrowed as he looked at her, but she could see the good humour in them. 'It's not a boy, is it?' he asked, squinting at her. 'You know, we didn't move halfway across the country just for you to meet a boy.'

Laughing, she shook her head. 'No, Dad. It's nothing like that. It's just someone sweet, who's in the same boat I am.'

The Grinkle Nonk

'The same boat? Is this person in a wheelchair too?'

Her smile receded a little; it became wistful along with her thoughts. 'No, not in a wheelchair exactly, but definitely disabled.'

His smile widened again as she lifted her bowl and drank the last of the cereal, that was mostly milk. She wiped her chin as he stood up. Leaning over the table he scuffed her hair again. 'Well, I'm happy for you,' he laughed, making his way over to the fridge. 'Just be careful, OK?'

'I will,' she replied as she grabbed her bag and wheeled her way out of the kitchen towards the front door. 'I love you, Daddy,' she shouted back.

'I love you too, sweetgums. I'll see you tonight!' he replied with a laugh, as he shook the mostly empty carton of milk from the fridge.

~~~~

They met where they'd agreed the day before, deeper into the woods than she'd ever been able to get to before. The Grinkle Nonk had flattened out a secret path for her so she would be able to get her wheelchair through the trees without any issues. It had then hidden the trail, hindering anyone from finding its home by accident. As agreed, there was a pile of stones next to an overturned log, and then behind the log there was the trail, just as it had told her it would be.

The Grinkle Nonk was as good as its word.

As she removed the brambles, she marvelled at how dark it was down the path. How the sun, hanging bright and warm in the morning sky, tried, but didn't quite succeed, to break through the heavy foliage overhead. She also noted how quiet it was. Suddenly, going to meet the Grinkle Nonk didn't seem like such a great idea. *What do I really know about this beast? I mean, I've listened to the songs, I've heard the stories about how ferocious, not to mention dangerous it is.* Her eyes darted back and forth, from the treetops blocking out the sun to the smooth, secret path cut especially for her chair. Everything seemed just right for her to walk, or roll, into a trap.

'You came,' the voice breathed from somewhere, hidden deep within the gloom. 'I didn't think you would.'

There was a rustle, and the bows of the trees bent as a huge shadow emerged from them.

It was the Grinkle Nonk.

Today, to her opened, not as scared eyes, it seemed much bigger than it had yesterday.

She opened her mouth to answer but closed it when she saw what was in its hands. It was the largest bouquet of flowers she'd ever seen. It consisted of colours that she didn't even know existed, and of blossoms she'd never seen before.

'I, erm … I made you this,' it stuttered, holding the flowers towards her. 'Just in case you came.'

'Of course, I was coming,' she said with a giggle, accepting the bouquet. It was far too big for her to hold in her chair, and she dropped some of them onto the trail.

The Grinkle Nonk laughed too. It was an odd sound, like a mixture of a pig squealing and an old diesel truck revving on a cold winter's morning. It made her laugh more.

'So, what are we going to do today?' she asked.

The beast grinned. To the untrained eye, the grin could have looked evil, malicious, as thick drool hung from its lower jaw, but to her it looked sweet. It couldn't help having protruding teeth, and four eyes that looked deep into your soul, any more than she could help being in a wheelchair.

'Have you ever climbed a tree?' it asked, shyly.

She chuffed and rolled her eyes. 'Once upon a time …'

'What?' it asked, cocking its head comically.

She laughed. 'Not in a long time,' she replied, banging her hand on the side of the wheelchair. 'This thing kind of makes it hard to do these days,' she quipped.

'Come with me, I'll take you to the tallest tree in the woods. We'll climb it together!' With that, the Grinkle Nonk headed down the dark path at a run.

She watched it go, disappearing into the gloom, becoming a part of the forest, that she thought must have been why it had been so good at surviving all this time. Part of her wanted to turn back, to go home and wallow in the comfort of her life with her mom and dad. To forget all about the Grinkle Nonk and maybe even make some human friends in this godforsaken town. However, the bigger part of her, the part that had made her such a great skateboarder, the part that pushed her down more and more exciting avenues, wanted to follow the beast.

So, she did.

As it turned out, she was glad she did.

~~~~

As Harper and the Grinkle Nonk disappeared down the dark lane, leaving a trail of flowers behind them, there were eyes on them. Envious eyes. They watched as the unlikely duo headed off into the dark woods.

Suzi knew the new girl was up to something. She hated the fact that it wasn't her who had befriended the Grinkle Nonk, that would have really been one over her sister. 'I bet they go picking flowers, or maybe even frolicking through fields together,' she spat. 'If it was me who had that thing as a pet, I'd use it to terrify my enemies, and help me get anything, and everything, I want.'

As she pouted, thinking these terrible thoughts, an idea began to form in her head. It was a plan, a diabolical one, one that would make her into a hero in this town and maybe, just maybe, even more popular than Agnes, her *beloved* sister. As she turned away from the hidden path, the plan was already evolving. A sly grin touched her lips. If there was any humour in it, then her brain had forgotten to inform her eyes about it.

7.

THE DAY WAS perfection. They climbed the tallest tree in the forest, it was bigger than any tree Harper had ever seen in her life. The Grinkle Nonk picked her, effortlessly, out of her chair and placed her on a branch so high up, she took a little dizzy turn. She'd forgotten how good it felt to be so far up a tree with the wind blowing through her hair. The Grinkle Nonk, or Nonk as she called it now, climbed after her, encouraging her higher. As it turned out, she didn't need much encouragement as the sharp tips of its antlers were only inches away from her bottom, and she didn't fancy feeling the sharp pinch of them spearing her rump.

At first, she was nervous climbing so high, but Nonk assured her it wouldn't let her fall. She gained more and more confidence with every branch.

After they conquered the tree, they went back to Nonk's lair. She was hesitant about this, the songs, and the stories of the killing and eating of people were still spinning through her head, on a never-ending loop. However, after seeing how beautiful the place was, the tales of viciousness and vileness were forgotten. The lair was huge. Half of it was underground, and the rest, above. The ceiling must have been at least twenty feet high. The walls were made from dried, impacted earth and roots that had been manipulated to look artistic, before being polished to a high sheen.

There were drawings on the walls. They looked like other Grinkle Nonks. There was one that stood out from all the others, it depicted a small, four eyed Grinkle Nonk holding hands with a larger one. She looked at it closer. 'Is that your mother?'

'Mother?' Nonk asked, cocking its head.

'Yes, mother. Is she the one who gave birth to you?'

An ugly smile, that was also rather sweet, overtook its face. 'Yes, mother,' it said, nodding and touched the drawing with a large claw.

'Did you draw it?'

Nonk nodded. 'It was in my head, so I put it on the wall. Do you like it?'

Harper nodded, wiping a tear from the corner of her eye. 'Very much so. Where's your mother now?'

Nonk looked at the picture and smiled again. 'Gone, with all the other Grinkle Nonks that came before. I'm the last,' it explained.

Harper wanted to hug Nonk now. *It must be so lonely here, all alone.* As she rolled towards it, second thoughts overcome her as she regarded the filthy fur matting of its body. 'I'm going to have to go home

The Grinkle Nonk

now,' she said, a smile brightening her eyes. 'I've had a lovely day. Should we do it again tomorrow?'

Nonk's eyes lit up. 'You mean you want to come to play again?'

Her smile widened. 'Very much so,' she nodded.

'You're not scared of me?' it asked, cocking its huge head. 'You don't think I'll eat you, like the other children do?'

She shook her head and reached out to his hand. 'No, I think you're very nice,' she said, squeezing its claw. 'But I do have to go now, maybe tomorrow we could go swimming.' *And I'll bring some soap,* she added in her head.

'I know a place. I go there to bathe, every year,' Nonk replied.

Harper was laughing as she began to wheel herself towards the door of the lair.

'I won't come down the track with you,' Nonk said as it stood by the entrance. 'I don't want to scare anyone, any more than I already have.'

Harper nodded and waved. 'OK Nonk. I'll see you tomorrow then,' she shouted wheeling her way out of the woods.

8.

'I SAW HER. She was with that *thing* from the woods. I'm telling you, she's bad news that one. Someone needs to have a word with her. She can't come waltzing into this town in her fancy wheelchair and befriend our oldest myth. It'll be the ruin of us all. If our parents find out that thing's real, they won't let us play anywhere near them woods again, you can believe that.' Suzi loved having the attention of a crowd, it made up for the attention she craved at home but didn't get because her parents doted on *perfect* Agnes. 'They went down a secret path, deep into the woods. It's my bet they've got some secret thing going on down there. Black magic, I'd say. Maybe they have children from other towns as slaves, or they're boiling them up to eat later, and make into glue.'

'Have you got any proof of this?' someone shouted from the crowd.

'You do know that people in wheelchairs can't waltz,' someone else shouted.

The Grinkle Nonk

Her face creased as she looked towards the voices. She ignored the second shout, of course she knew that people in wheelchairs couldn't waltz. 'No, I don't have any proof,' she spat. What do you want me to do? Follow them and maybe become their next victim?'

The boy who shouted shrugged and looked towards the rest of the crowd all around him. 'Well, kind of, yeah. At least get proof that she's with that thing.'

Suzi huffed. It had all been going so well until this *idiot* opened his fat mouth. 'OK then,' she replied, casting her evil eye out to him, hoping he would see it and bow to her will. 'I'll get the evidence you need. When I do, and you all believe me that she's in league with this devil, *then* we should do something about it. Are you with me?' She shouted the last words, hoping to whip the crowd into a frenzy. All she got for her efforts were mumblings and a lot of shrugged shoulders.

It didn't impress her at all.

~~~

That night, as she lay in bed, listening to her *perfect* sister snore in the next room, sleeping the sleep of the *perfect*, in her *perfectly* pink room. She couldn't sleep. Every time she closed her eyes, she saw the two of them together, that damned Grinkle Nonk and the stupid girl in the wheelchair.

Why is it not me? She shouted in her head, over and over, and over again. *Why did I not befriend that ugly, four-eyed beast? What's so special about her?*

As she tossed and turned, evading sleep at all costs, something began to hatch in her head. The plan she started to devise began to unravel before her.

It was a wonderfully horrible plan, but the more she thought about it, the more brilliant it became. She leaned over and flicked on the bedside light. She removed her little pad and pencil in her drawer and began to write in it.

It began with, Peggy and Prudence…

After a few minutes of intense scribbling, she put the pad down, turned off the light, and closed her eyes. She drifted off to sleep with a smile painted firmly on her face.

9.

THE POOL WAS glorious. It was cold, clean, fresh water, and it was deep. Nonk pushed Harper's chair into the shallows and held it as she levered herself out. The feel of the cold water against the heat of the morning was unbelievably good.

'I brought you a present,' Harper shouted as she swam into the deeper water.

'You brought a present for me?' Nonk shouted as it waded into the pool after her.

'Yeah, it's in that bag over there.' She pointed towards the white bag hanging on the back of her chair.

All its eyes widened, and its wet hair stood on end. 'No one has ever brought me a present before.'

'Well, considering what this present is, that doesn't surprise me one bit,' she laughed.

As Nonk reached the bag, its sharp claws tore it apart by accident, and a large bar of soap fell out onto the ground at its equally clawed feet. It looked at the soap, its eyes quizzical. 'What is it?' it asked.

'Soap.'

'Soap?'

She laughed. 'I knew you were going to ask that question. You rub it into your fur; it makes you clean and smell nice too.'

'Will it make me smell like you?' it asked, sniffing the bar that was now skewered on one of his claws.

'Kind of,' she shouted before ducking her head under the water. When she surfaced, Nonk was rubbing itself with the large bar. She laughed as the more it scrubbed, the more the white foam lathered all over it.

It looked at her, its red eyes scared. 'What's happening?' it roared.

'It's OK,' Harper replied. 'It washes off. Dunk yourself into the water and it'll float off.'

Nonk jumped into the deeper water and Harper was caught in a tsunami of soap suds. She screamed, ducking herself to evade the flotsam.

They played this way for most of the day, swimming, splashing, racing, and laughing.

~~~~

Suzi was watching.

The Grinkle Nonk

Every time the beast picked Harper up, she wished it would throw her out of the pool, onto the rocks at the far end. Then she prayed it would pounce on her and eat her... alive.

She was growing to hate this girl in the wheelchair.

No, hate wasn't the word she was looking for.

'Detest,' she snarled, baring her teeth, from where she was hiding, out of sight, in the trees. She'd followed her today, along the path, to this pool that she didn't even know existed, and she had lived in this town all her life. She hated that this new girl was having more fun than her. All she had was Prudence, Patty, and her horrible sister, Agnes, while Harper was having the time of her life with her very own monster.

'Well, we'll see about that,' she hissed as she climbed down from her hiding spot, just as the beast, now looking ridiculous covered in soap suds, ducked itself under the surface.

~~~~

'It's enormous!'

She articulated how big it was by waving her hands in the air. Prudence and Patty were her only audience this time, sitting before her on the grass of the field, nowhere near any trees. Their eyes wide as they hung off her every word.

You two are pathetic, she hissed in her head as she looked down her nose at the two adoring girls all the while keeping a fake, excited grin on her face. 'Its teeth are lethal; you can tell just by looking at them.'

Prudence and Patty both swallowed as they looked at each other.

'It has four eyes, and they are deep red. They're hypnotic too. Its got her in some sort of a trance. It tried to do the same with me, but I wouldn't allow myself to be taken under its spell. I'm far too strong minded for that. It is true, because why else would she be hanging around with such a stinking loser, and a dangerous animal? It needs to be stopped. We need to do something before something really *bad* happens.'

As she said the word *bad,* she in leaned closer, her wild eyes leering at both girls.

As they flinched, she continued her tirade. 'We need to convince the town that, first of all, this thing is real, and that secondly, it is dangerous. Luckily, I've got a plan. We're going into the woods. Prudence, you're going to bring your mum's big brown coat, Patty, we're going to need some tomato ketchup, or maybe soup…'

Both girls listened, in rapture, as Suzi explained the plan. There were smiles all around when she'd finished.

The Grinkle Nonk

10.

NO ONE HAD been back into the woods since the attack. No one had seen anything of the strange new girl, the one in the wheelchair, since they had stranded her in the clearing, at the mercy of the vicious beast. Half of the kids thought she'd been eaten, devoured, turned into soup for the Grinkle Nonk, the other half listened to Suzi, believing the girl was in cahoots with the animal and between them, planning something very wicked to be played out on the town.

Suzi was determined to convince them *all* of her theory. She knew Harper was still alive. She'd seen her with the thing in the woods, swimming and frolicking in the pool. 'OK, what we're going to do is this. Patty, you're going to climb on Prudence's back and drape that long coat over you both. Then I want you to attack me. I'm going to put my phone over here.' She placed the device in the branches of a nearby bush and set it to record video. 'You attack me. I'll fall over, and you rip my dress.

We'll show everyone the video, and the bruises I'll have, and all the kids will be on our side. You never know, this thing might even go viral.'

'Great plan,' Prudence gushed, grinning.

'Yeah, Suzi, I don't think anyone else could have come up with a plan as good as this,' Patty purred, as Prudence glared at her.

'Right then, get on her back and don't forget to make a lot of noise. You know, growling and all that stuff.'

'You want us to growl?' Patty asked, her voice rising at least three octaves.

'Yeah. It's got to be authentic too. It's a good job that I'm such a good actress because it looks like I'm going to have to carry this production on my own,' Suzi said, rolling her eyes.

As she turned, both Prudence and Patty pulled faces behind her back, sniggering. Patty pulled the coat over her head and Prudence, holding onto Patty's legs, staggered towards where Suzi was standing.'

'One, two, three … action,' Suzi shouted.

The girls began to growl and roar as they lumbered towards her. She turned towards the camera and screamed, throwing her hand up to her head, in what she thought of as a dramatic gesture. 'Oh no, it's the Grinkle Nonk! It's come back for me.'

Patty and Prudence made as much noise as they could, chasing after her, both girls doing their best to sound vicious, but were barely holding in their giggles.

'Argh, it's got me,' Suzi shouted, falling over.

Patty and Prudence then fell on top of her.

The Grinkle Nonk

'OK, OK, you can get off now,' Suzi ordered through a mouthful of dirt. She pushed the giggling monster, made up of her two best friends, off her. 'That should be enough,' she said, standing up, dusting mud and leaves from her dress. 'I'll edit it tonight, then we can show it to everyone tomorrow. Once they see this, they'll be convinced I was attacked by the monster. No one cares about Harper, she's new in town, but if *I'm* attacked, everyone knows me. They'll be angry enough to find and kill that beast!'

~~~

Later that night, while the world slept, Suzi edited her video. She blurred the monster into the background, so, to the casual observer, it would look ferocious and less like two girls with a fake fur coat over their heads.

She took her dress and ripped it, as if it had been attacked by claws. Then she went out into the garden with a sharp knife and found a large rock.

Sitting at the bottom of the garden, she held the knife in one hand, and the rock in the other. She knew what she needed to do; she just didn't want to do it. Closing her eyes, she thought about all the kids cheering her, as *Agnes* looked on from the wings. She grinned, everything she had ever wanted, was just a little bit of pain away from her grasp. Taking a deep breath, she put the knife to her skin and cut herself. It didn't hurt anywhere nearly as bad as she thought it would. She sliced into her skin again, and again, producing cuts that looked like she had been slashed at by an animal with terrible claws.

Once she was happy with the cuts, she bashed herself on the head with the rock. For a moment she saw stars, and different colours flash around her, before she did it again.

She ran into her house and looked in the mirror. There she was, covered in blood from superficial wounds, with a nice couple of bruises coming up on her face. Happy with her actions, she went to bed and dreamed of the Grinkle Nonk's head on a stick.

11.

'WHAT HAPPENED TO you?' was the question thrown at her from many different angles as she made her way into the park that had become the new playground.

'I ... I was attacked,' she stuttered breathlessly, flinging her hand to her forehead as her legs buckled beneath her. She flopped onto the grass, falling lightly.

Some of the boys ran towards her, and most of the girls too.

'Who was it?' the boy she still had a crush on asked as he leant in closer.

'It ... it was the ...'

Everyone was leaning in now. Their eyes taking in the rips in her dress and the blood from the wounds beneath them, as well as the black eye that was already turning a deep purple.

'It was the who?' the boy asked.

'The Who?' another boy replied, looking shocked. 'The band? My dad really likes them. Why would a band do something like this to a little girl? I've got to tell him to burn all of their records, right now.'

Suzi's eyes flared at the stupidity of the boy as he made to run off. 'It wasn't a band that did this,' she tutted. 'I was … the Grinkle Nonk!' As she spoke the name, she flung her hand to her head again, and pretended to faint.

Prudence and Patty looked at each other, grinning.

'The Grinkle Nonk, again?' Suzi's crush shouted.

Suzi grinned. The boy's name was John Thompson, his father owned the fishing tackle shop in town. She liked him and was quite sure that he liked her too. 'I have … a video,' she croaked as her mobile phone appeared in her hand. 'Look.' She sat up with a theatrical wobble and unlocked the phone. She clicked on a video, and all the kids gathered around, eager to watch the spectacle.

The picture was grainy and was filmed from an impossible angle for it to have been done on her own, but in the background was a beast that looked a little like two girls with a cheap coat over their heads, only it was so blurred no one could really tell. In the foreground, Suzi was fainting as the monster fell on top of her.

Everyone was silent as they watched the events unfold.

Suzi, Patty, and Prudence shared grins as the video was shared repeatedly to all the kid's phones.

The Grinkle Nonk

'Something needs to be done about this Grinkle Nonk,' John Thompson shouted, turning towards the other kids. 'And it needs to be done today. Who's with me?'

No one replied. Everyone just looked at each other, shrugging and mumbling.

'I'm with you,' Suzi, whispered, just loud enough for everyone to hear.

'We're with you too,' Patty and Prudence shouted, following their leader's lead. This was enough to provoke others in the crowd to join the band of vigilantes.

Soon, the whole park was with them. They were going to do something about the Grinkle Nonk menace, once and for all.

~~~~

Harper and Nonk were in a field she had never visited, or even seen before. It was vast and consisted of many different coloured plants, some of which were a mystery to her. The smells were amazing.

'Are you sure we're OK picking these flowers?' she asked.

Nonk looked up from where it had already picked a large bunch and nodded. It grinned a fierce grin, but Harper was used to it now and was able to read it perfectly. 'Yes. No one comes here other than me. I often come to smell the smells, usually when I'm sad, or lonely.'

Harper nodded as she watched Nonk pick some more. She'd lost her heart to this beast. It was so sad, stuck in the woods, all alone, just because of the way it looked. Just because it was *The Grinkle Nonk*. She wanted to wheel her chair over and hug it, tight, but it was just so enormous, it probably wouldn't even know she was there. It might even step on her by accident, squashing her flat.

She laughed at this image.

Nonk looked up, grinning again. 'What are you laughing at?' it grumbled.

'Nothing,' she replied and continued to pick the flowers.

~~~~

'So that's the plan,' a miraculously recovered Suzi was shouting to the crowd before her, bathing in all the attention. 'We make our way to its vile lair, and we *burn it down*. It's taken the new girl, Harper I think her name is, as its minion. She's living there with it. Think about this, before she turned up the Grinkle Nonk was nothing more than a legend, a myth, a story told so we would be home on time, so we would go to sleep at night, so we would eat up all our greens. Then this *Harper* turns up…' she spat the name. '…and suddenly, the monster is real. It's in *our* woods, doing God only knows what.'

Multiple shouts of encouragement came from the crowd, all of them started by Patty and Prudence.

'Let's gather supplies and burn it's lair down, hopefully with the vile thing inside. Who's with me?'

The Grinkle Nonk

This time, there was a roar from the gathered children. It seemed that everyone was with her.

'If Harper interferes, then we may have no other option but to burn her too. Who's with me on this?' Suzi shouted, raising her fist in the air.

Again, there was a rousing chorus of agreement.

She was satisfied, but she wanted one more thing. She wanted to make sure they were all fired up. 'Kill the beast,' she chanted. 'Kill the beast!'

It began as a whisper, but soon it was a song.

It wasn't long before it became an anthem.

She closed her eyes and listened. They were hers now, her own personal army. She breathed in the smell of the fired-up kids before her.

It was hypnotic. She hoped Agnes heard about this.

'Kill the beast! Kill the beast! Kill the beast!'

~~~~

Harper and Nonk were making their way back to the lair; they were laughing and joking. Nonk was pushing her with one huge arm while carrying what looked like half the field of flowers in the other.

She felt that life might be rather good, after all.

~~~~

They had jerry cans filled with petrol, mostly taken from their father's garages, or syphoned from some of the cars in town. They had sticks wrapped with rags, dipped in fuel. There were knives, pointed sticks, axes. John Thompson had even managed to steal a gun from his father's weapons cabinet.

They were ready.

'I know where it is,' Suzi shouted. Her normally bright blue eyes were blazing and seemed darker than usual.

She was drunk with power.

'Everyone, follow me.'

~~~

Nonk was heating up some nuts and berries they had foraged on their way back from the field. Harper was tidying up the lair and presenting the flowers about the room to help combat the stink she had slowly become accustomed to.

'Tell me, Harper. Why do you spend all your time with me?' Nonk asked as it pulled out a nut dripping in berry juice, to taste.

'Because you're my friend,' she replied.

'Yes, but shouldn't you be friends with the other children, and not a stinky old Grinkle Nonk like me?' it asked, licking the dripping juice from its teeth.

Harper stopped cleaning and looked at it. She smiled. The smile made her heart race in her chest. 'Nonk, you're my best... my *only*

The Grinkle Nonk

friend. I'd rather be here with you than with them other kids. I'm new in town, and I think I'm the only kid in a wheelchair they've ever seen.' She shook her head. 'I'm not one of them, Nonk. I don't think I ever will be.'

'But you're not a Grinkle Nonk either,' it replied, eating another berry-juice-covered nut. The dark jam dripped from its hairy chin.

'Then, we're the same. Don't you see? Both of us are outcasts, outsiders. We don't need anyone else to enjoy ourselves. We have each other.'

Nonk grinned and stuffed another nut into his mouth.

'Erm, do you want to let up on them?' she scolded. 'There won't be enough left for me.'

Nonk laughed. It was a loud, roaring laugh that made the trees outside the lair shake.

~~~

'Did you hear that?' John Thompson hissed, as he hunkered down in the bushes at the side of the secret path Suzi had exposed. He'd been walking next to her. They had almost been holding hands.

She had enjoyed that.

The roar rippled through the trees, sending flights of birds off into the sky, petrified by the bone shaking yell. Suzi shushed the rest of the group. 'We're near,' she whispered. 'It knows we're here. From here on in, we must be careful.'

Everyone agreed.

Most of them wanted to go home. A couple of them had experienced little accidents in their underwear at the sound of the roar, but none were willing to show their fear, so they continued, following their leader, even if they had to walk funny doing it. Once they reached the lair of the Grinkle Nonk, they would put the myth to rest. They would kill the beast and would become heroes in the town for years to come.

~~~~

Nonk threw a berry-covered nut towards Harper. She caught it in her mouth and crunched the tasty treat, allowing the juices to drip down her own chin. They were both laughing and covered in sticky red berry sauce.

Suddenly, Nonk stopped laughing. It raised its head and sniffed the air. Its four eyes flickering this way, and that, trying to find the source of the disturbance it had sensed.

'What is it?' Harper asked, a sudden nasty feeling in the pit of her stomach made her want to go to the toilet.

'I can smell people,' Nonk replied. As it looked at her, she noticed its wide eyes and flaying nostrils.

'It's nothing to worry about,' she soothed, but the quiver in her voice gave her away. 'I'm sure it's just some hiker lost in the woods. I'll go and look.'

Nonk nodded as Harper wheeled past him, out of the door and into the garden.

The Grinkle Nonk

There was no one there, the little clearing was empty. She turned, ready to go back inside, hungry for the tasty nuts and berries, when she saw the trees around the lair begin to wave and rustle. 'Who's there?' she demanded, sounding braver than she felt.

A girl emerged from the trees. She was wearing a ripped dress, and she had a black eye. Harper thought she recognised her from town but didn't know her name. From behind her came a boy. He was tall with wide shoulders; he was carrying a rifle.

Harper didn't like this, not one bit.

Then came the others. Kids she recognised from the clearing, although she couldn't put names to any of them.

'Oh my God, look at her,' another girl shouted as she emerged, carrying a sloshing red jerry can. 'She's covered in blood.'

Harper wiped the berry juice from her chin as she watched more kids appear from the trees. All of them were carrying weapons. She could see sticks, knives, and petrol cans. Some were carrying flaming torches, even though it was still daytime.

'See, I told you she was in league with that *thing,*' the lead girl shouted. Her face was a rictus of hate, of power, and of drunken glee. 'We're here for the Grinkle Nonk,' she continued. 'We're going to kill it, once and for all. Never again will it attack, and eat, the children of our town.'

Harper thought the speech sounded rehearsed. 'What?' she replied. The other kids were too occupied either looking at her wheelchair or the red berry juice all over her to notice that she'd shouted. 'What are you talking about? Attacking and eating children? Nonk has done no such thing. Sure, it's a beast, and a scary looking one too, but it's a gentle, lonely soul. It's polite and placid. We pick flowers, we go swimming. It's never once tried to eat me.'

'Nonsense,' Suzi shouted, interrupting Harper's speech. 'I've got a video of it attacking me. I've got the bruises, the torn dress, and the wounds to prove it. I can only assume you're in cahoots with this devil. We can see it in the blood all over you. You've sold out your own kind to collude with this monster.'

Most of the kids didn't know what *collude* meant, but they agreed with her anyway.

'Bring that filthy beast out here. Or we'll *drag* it out.'

Harper looked back into the lair; she could see Nonk hiding just inside. It was shaking, petrified of the crowd and their weapons. She turned back towards the leader. She didn't like that this girl's eyes were radiant with danger and her, too wide, smile was twitching. Nonk was in trouble. She needed to think of something, and fast.

'Bring the thing out,' Suzi demanded.

'Bring it out, bring it out …' the crowd began to chant.

Harper could taste the bad feeling in the air. Something was going to happen here, and it wasn't going to be good. The kids, all around the clearing now, were waving knives and flaming sticks. One boy had a gun.

'Listen … LISTEN,' she screamed.

The chant quietened, then stopped.

The Grinkle Nonk

'If I can get Nonk to come out here and introduce itself to you, will you all listen? You need to see it for yourselves. It's just a lonely beast, tired of being out here and tired of everyone being scared of it. All it wants to do is play and to have friends. Is that too much to ask?'

Suzi had a smug smile on her face; Harper wanted nothing more than to smack it off. However, she knew she was the leader of this motley crew and doing so would cause more problems than it solved.

Harper wiped her brow; she was surprised to see how much sweat there was to smear away. 'OK, listen. I'll bring it out, but you all have to promise to behave yourselves. Remember, its more scared of you than you are of it.'

A few of the kids lowered their makeshift weapons.

Thank God, she thought, with a sigh, glad to be able to breathe again. She turned back into the lair. Nonk was peeking through the door. *The poor thing looks scared out of its wits,* she thought. She smiled. It smiled back. She could see it was more than a little forced. Holding out her hand towards the beast, she coaxed it out of its lair. 'Come out here, Nonk. There's some kids who want to meet you,' she said.

~~~~

Suzi watched as the beast squeezed itself out of the entrance. Its head bigger than she'd remembered from back in the clearing, its teeth were larger and sharper, as were its claws. She noted that it was much bigger than she'd depicted in her video; she realised there was no way she would ever have survived an attack from that thing. None of this bothered her now, the other kids would have forgotten how it looked on her film once they saw it up close. She looked at John; he was looking back at her.

A wink and a raise of eyebrows flashed between them.

He looked around before secretly loading his gun.

Through hooded eyes, Suzi grinned; everything was going to plan. Today would be a day long remembered. They would kill the Grinkle Nonk and mount its head on the wall in the town hall and when her and John Thompson got married in a few years, after all they were only twelve and thirteen respectfully, they would display the beast's stuffed head as the centre piece on their wedding table, four eyes, and antlers, the lot!

She had her future mapped out before her, she just needed to get this little chore out of the way, and she could start living it. As the beast towered over her, it bent its head low, and twiddled its claws. *The stupid thing doesn't even know what to do with itself,* she purred in her head.

'Everyone, this is the Grinkle Nonk, but it prefers to be called Nonk,' Harper said, gesturing towards the shuffling behemoth.

Suzi noted the blood that had spilled out, all over the thing's mouth and down its chest.

She grinned; it was sly grin; it was a grin Agnes would have been proud of. Harper was walking the beast right into her trap.

'All it wants is to get to know you. It doesn't want to eat any …'

As Suzi shouted, 'NOW!' all hell broke loose in the little clearing.

12.

THE MORE HARPER tried to make sense of what was happening around her, the more she got confused. There was far too much happening for her to comprehend. She had witnessed the look between Suzi and the boy with the rifle. Her stomach had twisted, and the bad feeling she had when Nonk smelt the newcomers, intensified, but it was too late. Nonk was out of its lair and was next to her. Its head bowed, its claws twiddling.

She had a terrible feeling that she had led her friend into an ambush.

'NOW!' the girl who was their leader shouted.

This alerted Harper, and she watched as the boy pushed his way to the front of the crowd. It was all in slow motion as he raised the gun he was holding and pointed it at Nonk. He closed one eye and took aim at her large friend. That was when Nonk stepped forward with its hands in the air.

Harper thought Nonk was surrendering to the boy.

It wasn't until the report from the weapon startled her out of her reverie that she realised the gun was no longer pointing at Nonk. It was now pointing towards the ground, and the boy was upside down.

Rope had wrapped itself around his legs, and suspended him, leaving him dangling at least three feet in the air.

Harper gawped.

The rest of the kids were screaming. Chaos reigned as children, ran haphazardly, through the clearing. A frenzied panic had spread swiftly through the garden.

More of them were now swinging from their feet.

She looked for the young girl, the one who was their leader.

At first, she couldn't find her in the melee.

Then she did.

She was sitting on the ground, leaning forwards. Dark berry juice was spilling down the front of her dress, pouring from her mouth, and her nose. She was holding her neck, where more juice was gushing, pulsing, in an arc. The girl looked pale, sickly, almost like she might faint at any moment.

Kids were still screaming and swinging high in the trees, all of them dangling upside down, their arms hanging helpless over their heads.

She didn't know what to do.

All she could hear was a cacophony of sounds, screaming, laughing, shouting, growling.

She looked for Nonk.

The Grinkle Nonk

It too was running around the garden, obviously excited by the crazed events. Its blood red eyes were everywhere. It was covered in more of the berry juice, a lot more than it had been just moments ago.

It was ... laughing.

Eventually, the scene calmed, and Harper was able to see what was happening with more clarity. The children had all stopped running, they physically couldn't run anymore, as every single one of them were dangling, writhing, at the end of thick ropes, suspended from the trees. The only two who weren't, were herself and the girl who was their leader. She was still on the ground, the thick berry juice, that Harper now realised wasn't really juice, was still flowing from the deep gash in her neck. The pulsing was becoming slower, the arc not quite as long as it had been. Her body was twitching as dark red bubbles formed on her lips.

'Nonk, do something,' Harper gasped.

'OK,' it replied, stepping towards the girl. It flexed its claws and pushed them, slowly through her chest.

The girl coughed, just once. A rush of air was pushed from her mouth, accentuated by a pink mist that blew over the pretty flowers.

Nonk's huge hand pulled out of the girl, and her body flopped forwards. As she fell, her once radiant eyes found Harpers. All the power, all the greed, all the lust trickled from them. The pretty girl died in the fallen leaves, surrounded by pinecones, blood, her own intestines, and some lovely, pruned, blooming roses.

Nonk flexed its fingers once more and tore the girl's body apart as easy as if it was squashing an overripe peach.

Harper's eyes widened as it witnessed the girls head dislodge from the rest of her body, before splitting in two as a claw punctured it through her face.

Harper looked up at the grinning, blood beast before her. It smiled, thick globules of gore slid from between its teeth, falling at the wheels of her chair.

The monster then stepped over the decapitated, deflated body of the girl, towards where the boy who had the gun was dangling. He was still thrashing, trying to look up at Nonk from his upside-down disadvantage. It was all to no avail. The rope around his feet was too thick and tied in a slip knot, meaning the more he thrashed, the tighter the knot squeezed. He, along with the all the other kids, were neatly secured.

'No … no …' the boy pleaded.

Nonk flexed its claws again. 'Yes,' it replied in a guttural growl. It then slashed the boy's stomach. Just one slow pass was enough to tear through the clothes he was wearing and cut into the pale flesh of his stomach beneath. The sharp talons ripped through the boy's stomach as if it were a polythene supermarket bag. But this bag wasn't filled with groceries, this one was filled with steaming piles of intestine, raw meat, and blood.

Harper watched as steam rose from the boy's wounds. For some reason she remembered something she had read in a book about the Native Americans. That when they watched the steam rise from a fatal wound, they thought it was the man's spirit rising to become one with nature, and their ancestors.

The Grinkle Nonk

She no longer thought this was the case, not up close and personal.

She wanted to scream, but there was little, or no breath left in her to facilitate it.

With another, effortless slash, Nonk took the boys head almost clean off his upside-down shoulders. The bulbous appendage with the eyes bulging out of their bloody sockets, hung from the rest of the swinging body. It was secured only by the thinnest strands of flesh that were already stretching. A waterfall of blood rushed from the boy's torso, running over his lifeless head, and pooling on the ground, around the offal that had slipped from his stomach, beneath him.

Nonk laughed as it licked the boys steaming, fresh gore from its claws.

The screaming from other kids began again. Each of them, a witness to the murder and decapitation of two of their friends, all began crying, screaming, and thrashing on the ropes that were holding them tight, upside down, and helpless.

Harper couldn't move. Shock had paralysed her body, complimenting the uselessness of her legs. It took what little remaining breath from her body, and all the sounds from her head. All she could feel, taste, and hear was numbness.

Nonk moved from child to child. It slashed them, mauled them, disembowelled each and every one of them. It impaled them on its razor-like claws, tearing their limbs, biting off their heads. It opened up their stomachs and sucked out the innards of the hanging human pinatas.

When the screaming and crying stopped, and everyone was silently hanging, dripping from the trees, only then did Nonk begin to harvest the cadavers, piling them into macabre heaps in the middle of the pretty garden. Every now and then it would pick up a discarded organ, be it a liver, a kidney, or even a heart, and pop it into its mouth, chuckling in delight each time it licked the gore from its talon.

Four blood red eyes regarded Harper.

Nonk's teeth were scarlet. Entrails, intestines, and smeared, torn clothing hung from its mouth as it laughed.

Harper wanted, no, she needed to run, but of course, she couldn't. She was stuck, and even if she could run, there was nowhere to run to. The lair, the same lair where she and Nonk had frolicked and played less than ten minutes earlier, was now a human abattoir, a gruesome graveyard, a slaughterhouse scattered with the carcases and limbs of disembowelled children.

There was a red hue to the air as miniscule blood particles floated in the warm air eddies. She didn't want to breathe, because she knew that in the act of breathing, she would be consuming the children of the town's blood. It would make her just like the beast.

But she couldn't help it. She couldn't hold her breath for too long.

The air tasted of copper.

'Well, that should be enough to get me through the winter,' Nonk rumbled, approaching her. Its red eyes were wide, and where they had once looked sad, all she could see now was glee, gluttony, and a savage madness. It looked at her, its head cocked to one side, studying her. A smile broke on its face, one she used to find charming, even funny. Now, however, it was just sinister. 'Maybe just one more, little *something something*,' it grinned, picking gruesome remnants from its teeth. 'A small snack, as it were, before I sleep.'

'Nonk,' Harper gasped as her heart worked overtime in her chest. 'Why?'

The beast leaned in closer, all its eyes leered down at her. The stink of blood and, strangely enough, soap, hung heavy between them.

She inhaled the odd clean stench of death on its breath.

Its shoulders heaved as it chuckled. 'Have you ever heard the saying *a leopard cannot change its spots*?' it asked in the deep growl she had grown to love.

Harper's head bobbed as she nodded.

'Well ...'

It looked around the clearing, revelling in the mayhem, in the river of blood, the strewn innards all over the trees looking like perverse Christmas decorations, the piles of lifeless children, their accusing, dead eyes staring at her, demanding why she would do this to them.

It turned to look at her again. Its once sad eyes narrowed. It exhaled. As it did filth slopped from between its dangerous teeth.

It grinned.

Harper wanted to smile back, hoping that doing so might wake her from the nightmare she was currently having.

It didn't.

As she and Nonk stared at each other it grinned.

'Why?' she whispered.

'Because I'm the *FUCKING* Grinkle Nonk,' it roared.

With a flash of claws, a stab of hot, searing pain, and a slow blanket of agonising blackness draping over her, she realised she would never have to worry about making friends, or being stuck in a wheelchair, ever again.

The Grinkle Nonk

Ha ha ha, hoo hoo hoo
The Grinkle Nonk is coming for you
Ha ha ha, hee hee hee
The Grinkle Nonk'll eat you and me
He'll grind your bones,
He'll chew your head.
He won't stop biting till you are dead …

Ha ha ha, hee hee hees
The Grinkle Nonk lives in the trees
Hee hee hee, har har har
Tell your mum, you won't go far
Playing in the forest
Playing in the stream
There's no one around to hear you scream

The Grinkle Nonk
The Grinkle Nonk
The Grinkle Nonk
The Grinkle Nonk

D E McCluskey

The Grinkle Nonk

Authors Notes

So, this delightful little tale began life as a short rhyming tale I wrote in response to one of my favourite recent children's tales, The Gruffalo. There is a homage to this tale in the cover picture, just in case you have been living under a rock (or trapped in the Grinkle Nonk's lair) for the last ten years.

I have added the rhyme at the end of the book just in case anyone wants to read it.

I wanted this to be a nice little children's tale, that turns bad, very bad, on the last page, making the reader think twice about what the hell it is they have just read. I sincerely hope I have managed this.

It evolved into a short story, but because I just don't seem to be able to hone that skill, to keep a story below the seven-thousand-word mark, it has now developed into this little novelette that you have in your hands now.

I would like to be able to say that it is a social commentary on how the world is becoming shallow, and that social media is making us anything BUT social, but it's not. It's just a little tale about a monster, who is exactly what he looks like, a monster. The moral of the story is… if it looks like shit, smells like shit, tastes like shit… then it is probably shit!

A few *thank yous* that need to be mentioned.

D E McCluskey

Tony Higginson for his valued input. Lisa Marie Tone, for once again offering her excellent editing skills. Joe Matthews for the excellent cover art (let's see if were able to use it), and to Folklore Art for the alternative artwork, in case we can't use the main one.

Proof-readers, Kelly Rickard, Corrina Morse, and Lauren Davies… thank you ladies for your commitment to this.

But, most of all, as always, I need to thank the readers, the most important people in all of this madness. Keep reading, and PLEASE, PLEASE, PLEASE review!!!

Dave McCluskey
Liverpool
January 2022

The Grinkle Nonk

1.

It's a gruesome ugly monster,
Covered in hair and scales
For scaring naughty children,
Its story never fails
It swallows people down in one
Down in one fell swoop
Spitting bones to boil them up
To make some human soup

Naughty children everywhere
Are its favourite meal
But don't forget, it has been known
To make the good ones squeal
A rumble, roar, and shaking crunch,
A sloppy slurp and bonk
Tell-tale signs you're about to meet
The big bad GRINKLE-NONK

There stands an old dead oak tree
It's out there by the streams
It's said that Grinkle lives inside
And causes children's screams
Just pray it doesn't see you
Because no-one can survive
When it pins you down and skins you
Or eats you up alive

D E McCluskey

The grownups don't believe it
They know it can't be truth
They turned the story into the myth
For them to scare the youth
The older kids are not quite sure
This tale is a lie
They think that Nonk's a fairy-tale
Made up to make them cry

That's why the children run and play
All around that tree of wood
Running, jumping, shouting, laughing
Like only children should
Unafraid of all the monsters
Well, that's just how it seems
But none of them will play around
The dead oak in the streams

One small girl is sat alone
As she watches the children play
Determined that she'll not miss out
Or else she'll fade way
She is built a little different
From the other kids all there
She can't walk and has to sit
In her very own wheelchair

The Grinkle Nonk

2.

Oh, the children they include her,
They try to find a role
But your fun is very limited
When you're always stuck in goal
And the chair becomes a nuisance
When playing hide and seek
Because the mud sticks to the wheels
And causes them to squeak

So, there she sits all alone
A forlorn and lonely figure
Sat in goal and wondering why
That old tree's getting bigger
She wonders about the silence
The birds have stopped their singing
And what could be that horrid smell,
That to her nose is clinging

The other kids are standing still
Frozen there in fright
As a thing appears before them,
A most horrendous sight
There is stood, the Grinkle-Nonk
In all it's terrible glory
It's so much bigger in real life
Than described there in the story

D E McCluskey

Panic makes the children run
In each direction sprinted
While the chrome of our girl's special chair
Just caught the sun, and glinted
This glare caught the monster's eye
She was fixed now in its stare
Why, oh why had she been stuck
In this damn wheelchair

The monster slowly ambled forth
On the little girl advanced
While a million billion butterflies
In her belly danced
Could this be the end of her?
Was she now facing death?
Just what had it been eating?
To cause that stinking breath

"Hello there little squidgy girl",
The smelly monster said
Or could this be a hellish demon?
Cos surely she was dead
"My name it is the Grinkle-Nonk",
A thick voice it did boom
All at once she felt so dizzy
She fell into a swoon

The Grinkle Nonk

3.

When at last she came around
She was cold and all alone
One eye slowly opened up
With hopes that she'd be home
But all around all she could see
Were roots and old dead leaves
"I'm inside that old oak tree"
Her sobs now came in heaves

"Little girl, don't be afraid",
Came a gruff old voice
"You can leave anytime you want,
It really is your choice"
"You were cold and fell asleep
I just could not abide"
"To leave you in the woods alone,
So, I brought you inside"

"I know what I look like,
And I know that you are scared"
"But just before you run off home
I'd like to have a word"
"Loneliness and boredom
They drive me round the bend"
"When all I want in this whole world
Is just one good friend"

D E McCluskey

"Every time that I approach
I offer them a smile"
"But I am so big and scary
That folks they run a mile"
"It makes me feel so, so sad
Why is it do you think?"
"That I live in these dark woods,
And the reason that I stink"

"Would you be my little friend?
Please tell me, what's your name?"
For the little girl in the wheelchair
Life would never be the same
"My name is Harper, Mr. Grinkle-Nonk
Now, how do you do?"
"I'd love to be your friend and know
All there is to know about you"

From that day a friendship forged
They were thick as thieves
They played together every day
And rolled about in leaves
She didn't find him ugly
And he didn't mind her chair
They were new best friends, forever,
They played without a care

The Grinkle Nonk

4.

The children in the village
They worried about young Harper
They hadn't even seen her since
The day they met that troll
Wanting to know what was up
And how she spent her days
They followed her into the woods
They'd know, without delays.

Not one of them were ready,
For the shock that did amaze
For Harper and the Grinkle-Nonk
Could be summed in just one phrase
PURE FRIENDSHIP it did look like
From all that they could see
Laughing, playing, joking, frolicking
As close as close could be

They waited on her return
To ask about her friend
To enquire why the Grinkle-Nonk
Didn't bring about her end
She just laughed and told them
About his sad old plight
All he wanted was acceptance
He really was alright

D E McCluskey

"But he's ugly, big and scary,
And eats up kids for fun!"
"He's covered in hair with mighty claws,
And smells like a tramps bum"
"He may be all those things you say",
She replied now getting cross
"But you should all come and meet him,
If not, it'll be your loss"

The scene was set for the Grinkle-Nonk
To make his big debut
The children of the village all turned up,
There was really quite a few
Sitting in an underground room
With excitement in the air
When suddenly Poll came into view,
And everyone did stare

The Grinkle-Nonk had appeared,
This really was surreal
With Harper sitting next to him,
How proud could she feel?
"I'll thank you all for coming",
The Grinkle-Nonk he boomed
"You are very welcome to my lair,
Oh, and by the way… you're doomed"

The Grinkle Nonk

5.

There was one enormous roar,
And a shrieking shout
The kids were all up and running,
Only there was no way out
The Grinkle-Nonk was laughing hard
It was a nasty sound
As he grabbed the kids around him
And threw them to the ground

Some were eaten instantly,
Others left for later
They all gave Harper evil looks
Because they all did hate her
"Stop!" she cried at the top of her voice,
"Why do you need this feast?"
"Well, that's quite easy to explain,
It's because I'm a fucking beast"

"Harper, I really used you good,
But please don't think me rude"
"You see you children, all to me,
Are nothing but good food"
"Oh, my friend you've broke my heart",
Little Harper sobbed and said
"Ah well you will get over it!"
Then he bit right off her head

D E McCluskey

If you think about this tale
And are saddened by the sting
Or if you take nothing else from it
Let me explain one thing
The lines between right and wrong
Shouldn't be a quiz
If something's looking dangerous,
Then it very probably is...

Printed in Great Britain
by Amazon